For Monika

Copyright © 1993 by Nord-Süd Verlag AG, Gossau Zürich, Switzerland
First published in Switzerland under the title *Der neue Hund*
English translation copyright © 1993 by North-South Books Inc.

All rights reserved.
No part of this book may be reproduced or utilized in any form
or by any means, electronic or mechanical, including photocopying,
recording, or any information storage and retrieval system,
without permission in writing from the publisher.

First published in the United States, Great Britain, Canada,
Australia, and New Zealand in 1993 by North-South Books,
an imprint of Nord-Süd Verlag AG, Gossau Zürich, Switzerland.

Distributed in the United States by North-South Books Inc., New York.

Library of Congress Cataloging-in-Publication Data is available.
ISBN 1-55858-218-5 (trade binding)
ISBN 1-55858-219-3 (library binding)

A CIP catalogue record for this book is available
from The British Library.

1 3 5 7 9 10 8 6 4 2
Printed in Belgium

The New Dog

By Ingrid Ostheeren

Illustrated by Jean-Pierre Corderoc'h

TRANSLATED BY J. ALISON JAMES

North-South Books

NEW YORK

Flip and Woolly were lying on the front lawn when Carl drove up. The car door opened and out tumbled a panting yellow bundle of fur. It was a puppy!

"He's a purebred Golden Retriever," they heard Carl say. "Obedient, devoted, and easy to train."

"Did you hear that?" asked Woolly. "A devoted purebred!"

"Obedient too," growled Flip sleepily. Through half-closed eyes they watched the puppy.

"His name," Carl announced, "is Prince Bastian of Bennington."

"Ha!" snorted Flip. "He's even a *prince!*"

Prince trotted over to Flip and Woolly.
"Come and play with me," he said.
The dogs didn't even raise their heads.
"Are you obedient purebreds too?" he asked.
"Not on your life!" snarled Flip.
"We're just two lazy mutts!" added Woolly. "And
if you're clever you'll act just like us."

Flip and Woolly had lived happily on the farm with Carol for a long time. But then Carol married Carl and the trouble began. Right away Carl had tried to make the dogs do things—like sit, beg, or lie down. Of course, Flip and Woolly liked to do those things, just not when Carl told them to.

So Carl decided to get his own devoted dog.

"We may be in real trouble," said Woolly. "If Prince does everything he's told to do, it will make us look bad. And Carl might start trying to train us again, too!"

Flip growled, "No self-respecting dog should let himself be pushed around by a human. We'll just have to take over Prince's training and teach him to be a lazy mutt."

"I hope it will work," said Woolly.

"Trust me," said Flip.

Prince grew quickly. Carl worked hard training him—but Flip and Woolly worked hard too.

"Today I learned what to do when Carl says 'Heel!'" said Prince as he joined the other dogs by the pond.

"We've known that a long time," said Woolly.

"But we never do it," added Flip.

"Why not?"

"Because it's foolish. Once you do what he says, you're trapped. He says sit, you sit—even when you don't want to. It's better not even to start."

Prince understood. When Carl said "Heel," Prince stayed where he was.

Carl complained to Carol: "Something's wrong with Prince. I taught him to come when I call, and ten minutes later he wouldn't obey me."

A few days later, Prince proudly told his new friends, "I'm learning how to protect things now. It is very easy."

"That's good," said Flip.

"It is?" asked Woolly nervously.

"Trust me," said Flip with a wink. "Now, Prince, if you see something lying around, make sure you protect it. Don't let anyone come near! Nobody. Understand?"

Prince understood. When Mr. Wilson, the man who lived next door, put his suitcases outside and went back inside his house, Prince protected them.

Prince was getting to be quite a large dog, with a remarkable set of teeth, and he took especially good care of the suitcases. Nobody could touch those bags. Nobody! Not even Mr. Wilson.

So Mr. Wilson missed his bus to the airport. *And* he missed his flight to the Bahamas. Mr. Wilson was *very* angry. Carl was angry too. "That dog is unbelievably stupid," he said.

Flip and Woolly went to great pains to train Prince. They taught him how to chew slippers and how to dig up plants. They showed him how to snatch sausages and how to track mud across the clean kitchen floor.

"That dog is impossible!" said Carl, shaking his head at his wife.

"I don't think Carl likes me very much," Prince said sadly.

Woolly felt terrible. Maybe they had gone too far. "You should do something amazing to impress Carl," he suggested. "Show him that you're a real dog."

"What could I do?" asked Prince.

"I know," said Flip. "You're supposed to be a hunting dog. Go catch a bird and bring it to him as a gift."

Prince tried his best to catch a fat red hen. It was not so easy. The hens raced around, squawking wildly. Prince ran in circles, barking and snapping, trying to catch one. Then Carol came out—with fire in her eyes.

"She really yelled at me," Prince told his friends later. "I guess I'm stupid, just like Carl says."

Carl had taught Prince to fetch sticks.

"That's it!" said Flip. "If you want to impress Carl you get him the most beautiful stick you can find."

So Prince dug up the rosebush and proudly brought it to Carol.

She was furious. "This dog is a nuisance!"

"Prince isn't the dog I thought he would be," said Carl thoughtfully. "I guess we should get rid of him."

"This is the dog," said Carl to Mr. and Mrs. Miller.

They wanted to buy Prince for their granddaughter Sally.

"What a wonderful fellow. He looks remarkably intelligent," said Mrs. Miller. "Is he good with children?"

"Just watch," said Carl.

Sally ran across the meadow with Prince. She threw her ball up in the air and then ran to find it, laughing as Prince ran beside her.

Suddenly the ball landed in the river. When Sally tried to fish it out, she slipped and fell in. She couldn't swim!

"Oh no!" thought Prince. Although he was a Golden Retriever, he was afraid of water. But there was nothing else to do. He jumped right into the river, caught Sally's clothes in his teeth, and pulled her up onto the bank.

Everyone saw the whole thing.

"Now there's a *real* dog," said Woolly.

"A hero," said Flip.

"Your dog saved little Sally's life," said Mrs. Miller.

"He should get a medal!" said Sally.

"How much do you want for him?" asked Mr. Miller.

Carl looked thoughtfully at Prince. Then he looked at his wife. She was smiling.

Carl cleared his throat. "We've changed our minds. We're not selling Prince. I'm sorry to disappoint you, but we've realized how much a part of our family he is."

Carl lovingly scratched Prince on the head.

Prince trotted happily down to the riverbank.

"Guess what?" he said to Flip and Woolly. "I'm part of the family now."

"Of course you are," they said.

"Lie down with us," said Woolly. "It's time for a little nap."

Prince Bastian of Bennington made himself comfortable in the grass. He closed his eyes and listened to the whispering of the water. Just as he was about to fall asleep, Flip turned to him and whispered, "Do you think you could teach us to be brave? We want to be real dogs, just like you."